Frederick's Fables

A Treasury of 16 Favorite Leo Lionni Stories

Frederick's Fables

with an introduction by the author

Alfred A. Knopf
New York

For Pippo, Annie, Sylvan, and Gina

THIS IS A BORZOI BOOK PUBLISHED BY ALFRED A. KNOPF, INC.

Copyright © 1985, 1997 by Leo Lionni
All rights reserved under International and Pan-American Copyright Conventions.
Published in the United States of America by Alfred A. Knopf, Inc., New York, and
simultaneously in Canada by Random House of Canada Limited, Toronto.
Distributed by Random House, Inc., New York. This edition is an expanded version
of a work originally published by Pantheon Books, a division of Random House,
Inc., in 1985.

http://www.randomhouse.com/

Library of Congress Cataloging-in-Publication Data
Lionni, Leo, 1910– .
Frederick's fables : a treasury of 16 favorite Leo Lionni stories / with an
introduction by the author. — [Rev. ed.]
p. cm.
Reprint of words originally published 1960–1994 with a new introduction and three
added stories.
Contents: Frederick — Fish is fish — Alexander and the wind-up mouse — The
biggest house in the world — Geraldine, the music mouse — Tico and the golden
wings — Cornelius — Swimmy — In the rabbitgarden — Theodore and the talking
mushroom — A color of his own — The greentail mouse — The alphabet tree —
Matthew's dream — Six crows — An extraordinary egg.
1. Children's stories, American. [1. Animals—Fiction. 2. Short stories.] I. Title.
PZ7.L6634Fr   1997
[E]—dc21   97-9906

ISBN 0-679-88826-8 (trade)
        0-679-98826-2 (lib. bdg.)

Printed in the United States of America

10 9 8 7 6 5 4 3 2 1

Contents

Me as in Mouse

I must confess that I always feel somewhat embarrassed when I am introduced as a children's book author. Not because I consider the making of picture books a minor art form and would prefer my name to be associated with more ponderous activities in the field of Art. Nor because I made my first book at the ripe old age of fifty. Nor because it happened as casually as it did.

My reluctance probably has its origin in my early childhood, when my first defiant answer to the question "What do you want to be when you grow up?" was "The bell of the trolley car." A few years later, and somewhat wiser, I came up with a more reasonable response: "I want to be an artist." That would still be my answer today.

At the time, we lived in Amsterdam, just a few steps from two of the most wonderful museums of the world, the Rijksmuseum and the Stedelijk. There I spent many a Sunday, drawing from plaster casts of Greek sculptures and looking with awe not only at the paintings and drawings of Rembrandt and Velázquez but also at the abstract works of Mondrian and Klee.

And then there were the copyists, with their gray smocks soiled with paint, an open paint box at their feet, a palette in the left hand and a delicate brush in the other. Breathless, I would watch them as they moved slowly in front of their easels, performing, almost invisibly, stroke by stroke, the magic of duplication. They were the first real painters I had ever seen. It is surely from them that I learned to cock my head when weighing the success or failure of a touch of burnt umber. It was probably then, as I stood there spellbound, and like the artist, unaware of the people around me, that I discovered the creative delights of craftsmanship, and the pleasure of recognizing the solidity of one's lonely self in the midst of a crowd.

I learned about design by helping my Uncle Piet, who was a young architect, with menial drafting tasks. And at home I would listen, whether I wanted to or not, to my mother, an extraordinary soprano, practice a Mozart aria or a Schubert lied. Painting, sculpture, architecture, design, and music, old and new, all came under the same heading: Art. And I wanted to be an artist.

Today, as then, I am involved in all the arts. I paint, I sculpt, I design. I write. Much of it to the sound of Mozart and Schubert. What tempts, excites, and motivates me is the underlying unity of the arts, their many surprising connections and cross-references, and the central poetic charge they share.

Such an eclectic attitude may well seem to be dispersive. And indeed I sometimes wonder if it would not have been better to devote all my time and energies to one well-defined profession. But in retrospect I am happy to have lived so intensely my adventure with all the arts. Not to claim the status of a "real professional" in any one endeavor has been a small price to pay for the many benefits and pleasures of trespassing.

It now seems strange to me that my incursion into the open sunny field of children's books happened when it did, late in life, for no art form benefits as much from the total experience in the arts as the picture book. No wonder that when I entered the field I knew that I was walking on familiar ground.

It happened in a most casual manner on a crowded commuter train from New York, where I worked, to Greenwich, Connecticut, where we lived. With me were my two restless grandchildren Annie and Pippo, who had come to spend the weekend with us. To keep them quiet and well behaved was not an easy job. After all the strategies of reasonable persuasion had failed, I had an idea. From the ad pages of *Life* magazine, I tore a few small pieces of colored paper and improvised a story—the adventures of two round blobs of color, one blue, the other yellow, who were inseparable friends and who, when they embraced, became green. The children were glued to their seats, and after the happy end I had to start all over again. That evening at home I made a rough dummy.

My friend Fabio Coen, then children's book editor for Obolensky, Inc., saw *Little Blue and Little Yellow* when he came for dinner at our house the very next day, and decided then and there to have it published.

I had been lucky.

That was thirty-eight years ago. Now Annie is an architect and Pippo is a graphic designer in Paris. And I have just given birth to my fortieth picture book.

Where *do* ideas come from? Authors of children's books well know how frequently the question is asked. It implies the naive assumption that authors have the key to a bottomless reservoir of stories as yet untold, and that they possess a highly specialized mechanism to retrieve them.

Nothing could be further from the truth. To trap the incredibly complex mental process that shapes the development of a story from birth to full-fledged maturity is a hopeless task. As it moves forward from word to word, from image to image, from page to page, a story leaves but the vaguest traces of its tortuous itinerary, and at the end the glowing, solid reality of the finished work all but obliterates the long travail that brought it to its satisfying conclusion. Time and again have I tried to identify the thoughts, feelings, or events that triggered an "idea" into being. Of my many books, I have succeeded in tracing but a few to the possible circumstances of their birth. *Frederick, Swimmy*, and *Cornelius* are among these exceptions. They show how fortuitous and fragile those circumstances are, and how difficult it is to answer the question "Where do you get your ideas, Mr. Lionni?"

In the early sixties, we were living in the hills above the small resort town of Lavagna on the Italian Riviera. The house, a pink stuccoed cube typical of the area, sat in the midst of terraced vineyards and dense olive groves, and from the windows the view embraced the spectacular Tigullio Bay with Sestri Levante to the east and Portofino to the west.

The studio was an adjacent reconverted barn. One sunny afternoon, on my way to work, I found myself face-to-face (or foot-to-face) with a very frightened little field mouse. When it saw me, it froze on its tiny feet. Then it jumped up and darted into the geraniums that flanked the flagstone path.

It was a warm day. The air was filled with the heavy scent of magnolias and orange blossoms and the monotonous sound of crickets. Far below in the hazy sunlight the ocean quivered slightly. I decided to take a nap.

As I lay on my couch, my thoughts began to meander in ever-widening circles. I woke up an hour or so later from a heavy sleep, incapable of moving. As I lay there motionless on my side, my eyes wandered along the shelves of my studio, which were filled not only with books but with hundreds of objects I had collected on my travels around the world. "How much nonsense," I thought. And I found myself saying (I still remember the words), "Once upon a time there was a little field mouse. All the other mice gathered nuts and berries for the winter ahead, while he collected pebbles. 'Why do you collect pebbles?' the others asked, annoyed. 'You never know. They may come in handy someday,' he answered mysteriously."

When I got up, I went about my business without giving that fantasy or my encounter with the mouse another thought. But I remembered a few weeks later when I began working on the story of *Frederick*, which then seemed to have appeared from nowhere.

Way back in the early fifties, we spent a month in Menemsha on Martha's Vineyard. One day I stood on a mooring in the little harbor waiting for a friend to pick me up with his boat when, in the water below, I saw a school of glittering minnows idly moving about. Suddenly, there was the roar of an outboard motor. Closing ranks, the minnows swiftly swerved around and, like one big fish, disappeared in the dark of the deeper water. They reappeared several years later at the surface of my memory as *Swimmy* and his friends.

Cornelius was born from a doodle I drew during a long and tedious telephone conversation. It is not surprising that it should have been the drawing of a lizard, because our garden is inhabited by hundreds of the playful little animals, who congregate in the warm hours of the day on the flagstones of the path to my studio. Absentmindedly, as I listened and talked, I drew one. It was standing on its hind legs like a miniature dinosaur. Without knowing why, I added a zigzag line to its back, and then when I finished the call, I threw the doodle into the wastepaper basket. But almost immediately I retrieved it, smoothed the wrinkles, and looked at it, letting my thoughts wander. Again, as with *Frederick*, words came to my mind, this time a title: "The Crocodile Who Walked Upright." It later became "Richard, the Upright Crocodile" and still later, when the text had been written and the pictures drawn, simply *Cornelius*.

It would be nice to know how the little mouse on the path to my studio began collecting pebbles and later became Frederick, a poet who collects sunrays, colors, and words; how a school of fish became the friends of Swimmy, a political idealist; and how the doodle of a lizard grew into Cornelius, a crocodile who saw and changed the world because he walked upright. For better or for worse, the steps and leaps of the imagination escape the mechanics of our memory and our understanding. The little we *do* know is that somehow in the flow of thoughts that endlessly fill our minds, the artist learns to recognize, capture, and remember that which is useful to his purpose.

Now you may ask yourself why I titled this piece *"Me* as in Mouse." The answer is simple: I wanted to stress the point that, like all fiction, illustrated children's books are inevitably autobiography.

I have mentioned some minor incidents of my own life that have triggered the ideas for my fables. What I did not mention is the fact that without delving deep into the distant memories of their own childhoods, authors could not find the mood, the tone, the imagery that characterize their books. They could not create convincing protagonists were they not able to fully identify with their heroes, a quality they inherit from their early youth.

If, in that sense, Frederick, Cornelius, and all the others are me, then Swimmy is perhaps the most pertinent example. Little by little, conditioned by the events of his life, he discovers the meaning of beauty as a life force and finally assumes his role as the eye who sees for the others. "I'll be the eye," he says.

Like Swimmy, the creator of picture books for children has the responsibility to see for the others. He has the power and hence the mission to reveal beauty and meaning. A good picture book should have both.

Come to think of it, would "I as in Eye" have been a better title?

Leo Lionni

Frederick

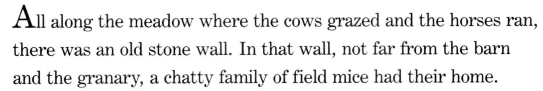

All along the meadow where the cows grazed and the horses ran, there was an old stone wall. In that wall, not far from the barn and the granary, a chatty family of field mice had their home.

But the farmers had moved away, the barn was abandoned, and the granary stood empty. And since winter was not far off, the little mice began to gather corn and nuts and wheat and straw. They all worked day and night.

All—except Frederick.

"Frederick, why don't you work?" they asked.

"I _do_ work," said Frederick. "I gather sunrays for the cold dark winter days."

And when they saw Frederick sitting there, staring at the meadow, they said, "And now, Frederick?"

"I gather colors," answered Frederick simply. "For winter is gray."

And once Frederick seemed half asleep. "Are you dreaming, Frederick?" they asked reproachfully.

But Frederick said, "Oh no, I am gathering words. For the winter days are long and many, and we'll run out of things to say."

The winter days came, and when the first snow fell, the five little field mice took to their hideout in the stones. In the beginning there was lots to eat, and the mice told stories of foolish foxes and silly cats. They were a happy family.

But little by little they had nibbled up most of the nuts and berries, the straw was gone, and the corn was only a memory. It was cold in the wall and no one felt like chatting.

Then they remembered what Frederick had said about sunrays and colors and words. "What about *your* supplies, Frederick?" they asked.

"Close your eyes," said Frederick as he climbed onto a big stone. "Now I send you the rays of the sun. Do you feel how their golden glow . . ."

And as Frederick spoke of the sun the four little mice began to feel warmer. Was it Frederick's voice? Was it magic?

"And how about the colors, Frederick?" they asked anxiously.

"Close your eyes again," Frederick said. And when he told them of the blue periwinkles, the red poppies in the yellow wheat, and the green leaves of the berry bush, they saw the colors as clearly as if they had been painted in their minds.

"And the words, Frederick?"

Frederick cleared his throat, waited
a moment, and then, as if from
a stage, he said:

8

"Who scatters snowflakes? Who melts the ice?
Who spoils the weather? Who makes it nice?
Who grows the four-leaf clovers in June?
Who dims the daylight? Who lights the moon?

Four little field mice who live in the sky.
Four little field mice . . . like you and I.
One is the Springmouse who turns on the showers.
Then comes the Summer who paints in the flowers.
The Fallmouse is next with walnuts and wheat.
And Winter is last . . . with little cold feet.

Aren't we lucky the seasons are four?
Think of a year with one less . . . or one more!"

When Frederick had finished, they all applauded. "But Frederick," they said, "you are a poet!"

Frederick blushed, took a bow, and said shyly, "I know it."

Fish Is Fish

At the edge of the woods there was a pond, and there a minnow and a tadpole swam among the weeds. They were inseparable friends.

One morning the tadpole discovered that during the night he had grown two little legs.

"Look," he said, triumphantly. "Look, I am a frog!"

"Nonsense," said the minnow. "How could you be a frog if only last night you were a little fish, just like me!"

They argued and argued until finally the tadpole said, "Frogs are frogs and fish is fish and that's that!"

In the weeks that followed, the tadpole grew tiny front legs and his tail got smaller and smaller. And then one fine day, a real frog now, he climbed out of the water and onto the grassy bank.

The minnow too had grown and had become a full-fledged fish. He often wondered where his four-footed friend had gone. But days and weeks went by and the frog did not return.

Then one day, with a happy splash that shook the weeds, the frog jumped into the pond.

"Where have you been?" asked the fish excitedly.

"I have been about the world—hopping here and there," said the frog, "and I have seen extraordinary things."

"Like what?" asked the fish.

"Birds," said the frog mysteriously. "Birds!" And he told the fish about the birds, who had wings, and two legs, and many, many colors.

As the frog talked, his friend saw the birds fly through his mind like large feathered fish.

"What else?" asked the fish impatiently.

"Cows," said the frog. "Cows! They have four legs, horns, eat grass, and carry pink bags of milk.

"And people!" said the frog. "Men, women, children!" And he talked and talked until it was dark in the pond.

But the picture in the fish's mind was full of lights and colors and marvelous things, and he couldn't sleep. Ah, if he could only jump about like his friend and see that wonderful world.

And so the days went by. The frog had gone and the fish just lay there dreaming about birds in flight, grazing cows, and those strange animals, all dressed up, that his friend called people.

One day he finally decided that come what may, he too must see them. And so with a mighty whack of the tail he jumped clear out of the water and onto the bank. He landed in the dry, warm grass and there he lay gasping for air, unable to breathe or to move. "Help," he groaned feebly.

Luckily the frog, who had been hunting butterflies nearby, saw him and with all his strength pushed him back into the pond.

Still stunned, the fish floated about for an instant. Then he breathed deeply, letting the clean, cool water run through his gills. Now he felt weightless again, and with an ever-so-slight motion of the tail he could move to and fro, up and down, as before.

The sunrays reached down within the weeds and gently shifted patches of luminous color. This world was surely the most beautiful of all worlds. He smiled at his friend the frog, who sat watching him from a lily leaf. "You were right," he said. "Fish is fish."

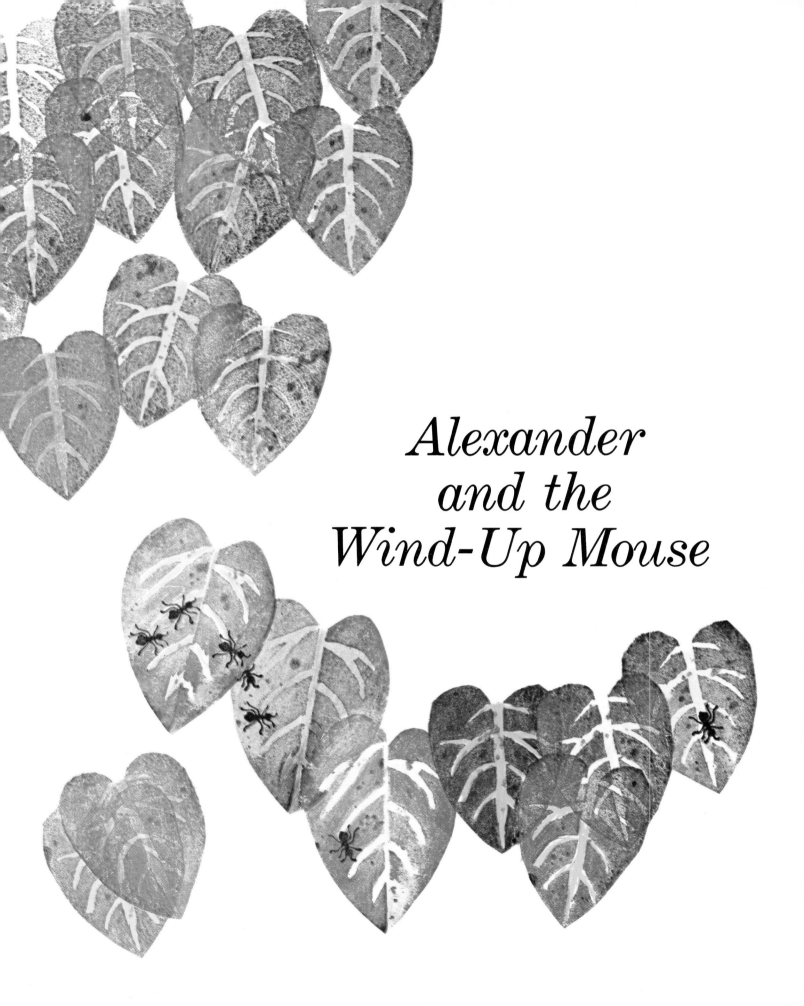

Alexander
and the
Wind-Up Mouse

"Help! Help! A mouse!" There was a scream. Then a crash. Cups, saucers, and spoons were flying in all directions.

Alexander ran for his hole as fast as his little legs would carry him. All he wanted was a few crumbs, and yet every time they saw him they would scream for help or chase him with a broom.

One day, when there was no one in the house, Alexander heard a squeak in Annie's room. He sneaked in and what did he see? Another mouse. But not an ordinary mouse like himself. Instead of legs it had two little wheels, and on its back there was a key.

"Who are you?" asked Alexander.

"I am Willy the wind-up mouse, Annie's favorite toy. They wind me to make me run around in circles, they cuddle me, and at night I sleep on a soft white pillow between the doll and a woolly teddy bear. Everyone loves me."

"They don't care much for me," said Alexander sadly. But he was happy to have found a friend. "Let's go to the kitchen and look for crumbs," he said.

"Oh, I can't," said Willy. "I can only move when they wind me. But I don't mind. Everybody loves me."

Alexander, too, came to love Willy. He went to visit him whenever he could. He told him of his adventures with brooms, flying saucers, and mousetraps. Willy talked about the penguin, the woolly bear, and mostly about Annie. The two friends spent many happy hours together.

But when he was alone in the dark of his hideout, Alexander thought of Willy with envy.

"Ah!" he sighed. "Why can't I be a wind-up mouse like Willy and be cuddled and loved."

One day Willy told a strange story. "I've heard," he whispered mysteriously, "that in the garden, at the end of the pebblepath, close to the blackberry bush, there lives a magic lizard who can change one animal to another."

"Do you mean," said Alexander, "that he could change me into a wind-up mouse like you?"

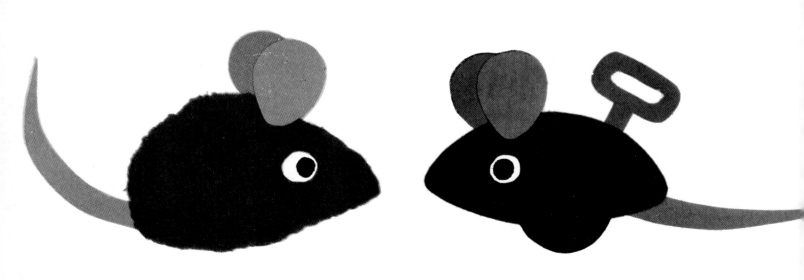

That very afternoon Alexander went into the garden and ran to the end of the path. "Lizard, lizard," he whispered. And suddenly there stood before him, full of the colors of flowers and butterflies, a large lizard. "Is it true that you could change me into a wind-up mouse?" asked Alexander in a quivering voice.

"When the moon is round," said the lizard, "bring me a purple pebble."

For days and days Alexander searched the garden for a purple pebble. In vain. He found yellow pebbles and blue pebbles and green pebbles—but not one tiny purple pebble.

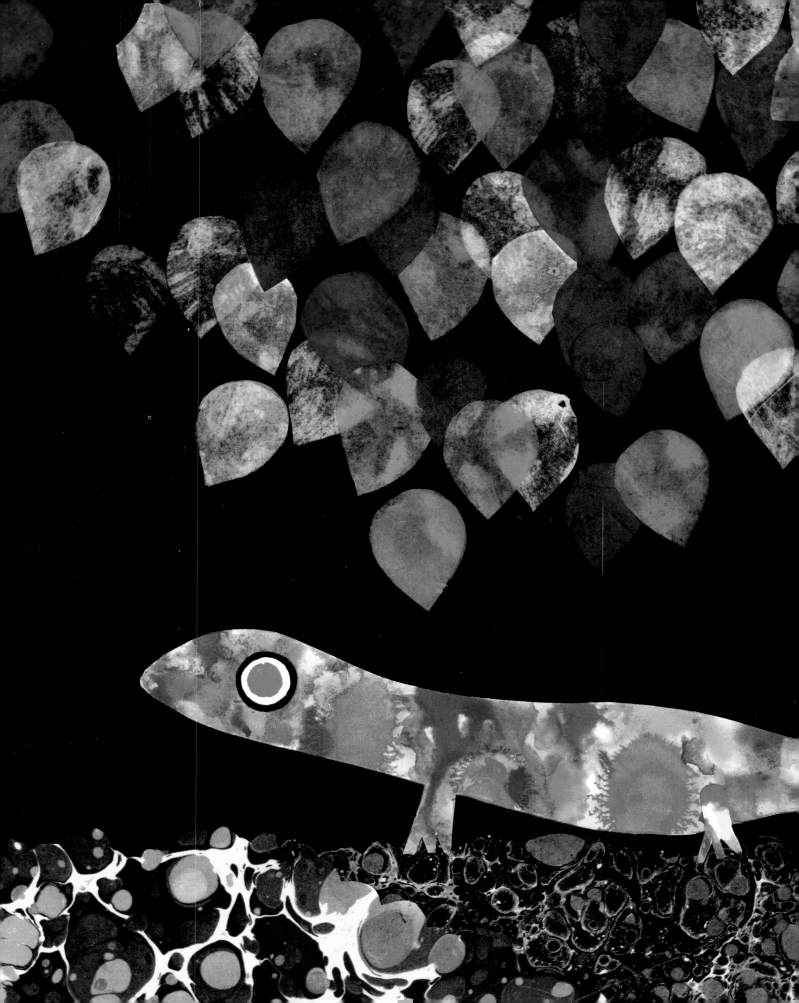

At last, tired and hungry, he returned to the house. In a corner of the pantry he saw a box full of old toys, and there, between blocks and broken dolls, was Willy. "What happened?" said Alexander, surprised.

Willy told him a sad story. It had been Annie's birthday. There had been a party and everyone had brought a gift. "The next day," Willy sighed, "many of the old toys were dumped in this box. We will all be thrown away."

Alexander was almost in tears. "Poor, poor Willy!" he thought. But then suddenly something caught his eye. Could it really be . . . ? Yes, it was! It was a little purple pebble.

All excited, he ran to the garden, the precious pebble tight in his arms. There was a full moon. Out of breath, Alexander stopped near the blackberry bush. "Lizard, lizard, in the bush," he called quickly.

The leaves rustled and there stood the lizard. "The moon is round, the pebble found," said the lizard. "Who or what do you wish to be?"

"I want to be . . . " Alexander stopped. Then suddenly he said, "Lizard, lizard, could you change Willy into a mouse like me?"

The lizard blinked. There was a blinding light. And then all was quiet. The purple pebble was gone.

Alexander ran back to the house as fast as he could. The box was there, but alas it was empty. "Too late," he thought, and with a heavy heart he went to his hole in the baseboard.

Something squeaked! Cautiously Alexander moved closer to the hole. There was a mouse inside. "Who are you?" said Alexander, a little frightened.

"My name is Willy," said the mouse.

"Willy!" cried Alexander. "The lizard . . . the lizard did it!" He hugged Willy and then they ran to the garden path. And there they danced until dawn.

The Biggest House
in the World

Some snails lived on a juicy cabbage. They moved gently around, carrying their houses from leaf to leaf, in search of a tender spot to nibble on.

One day a little snail said to his father, "When I grow up I want to have the biggest house in the world."

"That is silly," said his father, who happened to be the wisest snail on the cabbage.

"Some things are better small."

And he told this story.

33

Once upon a time, a little snail, just like you, said to his father, "When I grow up I want to have the biggest house in the world."

"Some things are better small," said his father. "Keep your house light and easy to carry."

But the little snail would not listen, and hidden in the shade of a large cabbage leaf, he twisted and twitched, this way and that, until he discovered how to make his house grow.

It grew and grew, and the snails on the cabbage said, "You surely have the biggest house in the world."

The little snail kept on twisting and twitching until his house was as big as a melon. Then, by moving his tail swiftly from left to right, he learned to grow large pointed bulges. And by squeezing and pushing, and by wishing very hard, he was able to add bright colors and beautiful designs.

Now he knew that his was the biggest and the most beautiful house in the whole world. He was proud and happy.

A swarm of butterflies flew overhead.

"Look!" one of them said. "A cathedral!"

"No," said another, "it's a circus!"

They never guessed that what they were looking at was the house of a snail.

And a family of frogs, on their way to a distant pond, stopped in awe. "Never," they later told some cousins, "never have you seen such an amazing sight. An ordinary little snail with a house like a birthday cake."

One day, after they had eaten all the leaves and only a few knobby stems were left, the snails moved to another cabbage. But the little snail, alas, couldn't move. His house was much too heavy.

He was left behind, and with nothing to eat he slowly faded away. Nothing remained but the house. And that too, little by little, crumbled, until nothing remained at all.

That was the end of the story. The little snail was almost in tears.

But then he remembered his own house. "I shall keep it small," he thought, "and when I grow up I shall go wherever I please."

And so one day, light and joyous, he went on to see the world.

Some leaves fluttered lightly in the breeze, and others hung heavily to the ground. Where the dark earth had split, crystals glittered in the early sun. There were polka-dotted mushrooms, and towery stems from which little flowers seemed to wave. There was a pine cone lying in the lacy shade of ferns, and pebbles in a nest of sand, smooth and round like the eggs of the turtledove. Lichen clung to the rocks and bark to the trees. The tender buds were sweet and cool with morning dew.

The little snail was very happy.

The seasons came and went, but the snail never forgot the story his father had told him. And when someone asked, "How come you have such a small house?" he would tell the story of *the biggest house in the world.*

Geraldine, the Music Mouse

Geraldine had never heard music before. Noises, yes. Many noises—the voices of people, the slamming of doors, the barking of dogs, the rushing of water, the meows of cats in the courtyard. And, of course, the soft peeping of mice. But music, never.

Then one morning . . .

In the pantry of the empty house where Geraldine lived, she discovered an enormous piece of Parmesan cheese—the largest she had ever seen. Eagerly, she took a little bite from it. It was delicious. But how would she be able to take it to her secret hideout in the barn?

She ran to her friends who lived next door and told them about her discovery. "If you help me carry it to my hideout," she said, "I'll give each of you a big piece."

Her friends, who loved cheese, happily agreed. "Let's go!" they said. And off they went.

"It's enormous! It's gigantic! It's immense! It's fantastic!" they shouted with joy when they saw the piece of cheese. They pushed and pulled and tugged and finally they managed to carry it to Geraldine's hideout.

There, Geraldine climbed to the very top of the cheese. She dug her little teeth into it and pulled away crumb after crumb, chunk after chunk.

As her friends carried away their cheese tidbits, Geraldine peered in amazement at the hole she had gnawed. There she saw the shapes of two enormous ears—cheese ears!

As soon as her friends were gone, she went back to work again, nibbling away at the cheese as fast as she could. When she was halfway through, Geraldine climbed down to have a look at the forms she had freed. She could hardly believe what she saw. The ears were those of a giant mouse, still partly hidden, of solid cheese. To its puckered lips it held a flute. Geraldine gnawed and gnawed until she had finally uncovered the entire mouse.

Then she realized that the flute was really the tip of the mouse's tail. Astonished, exhausted, and a little frightened, Geraldine stared at the cheese statue. With the dimming of the last daylight she fell asleep.

Suddenly she was awakened by some strange sounds. They seemed to come from the direction of the mouse's flute. She jumped to her feet. As it grew darker, the sounds became clearer and more melodious until they seemed to move lightly through the air like invisible strings of silver and gold. Never had Geraldine heard anything so beautiful.

"Music!" she thought. "This must be music!"

She listened all through the night until the first glow of dawn filtered through the dusty windowpanes. But as the cheese mouse was slowly bathed in light, the music became softer, until it stopped altogether.

"Play, play," Geraldine begged. "Play some more!"

But not a sound came from the flute.

"Will it ever play again?" Geraldine thought as she gobbled up some of the crumbs that lay around.

When the next evening approached, it brought the answer to her question. The music began faintly at dusk and lasted until the break of day. And so, night after night, the cheese flutist played for Geraldine. She learned to recognize the melodies, and even in daylight they lingered in her ears.

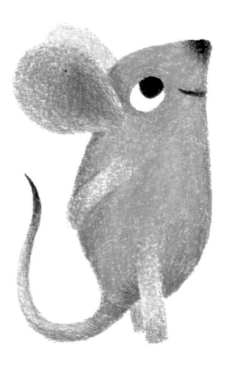

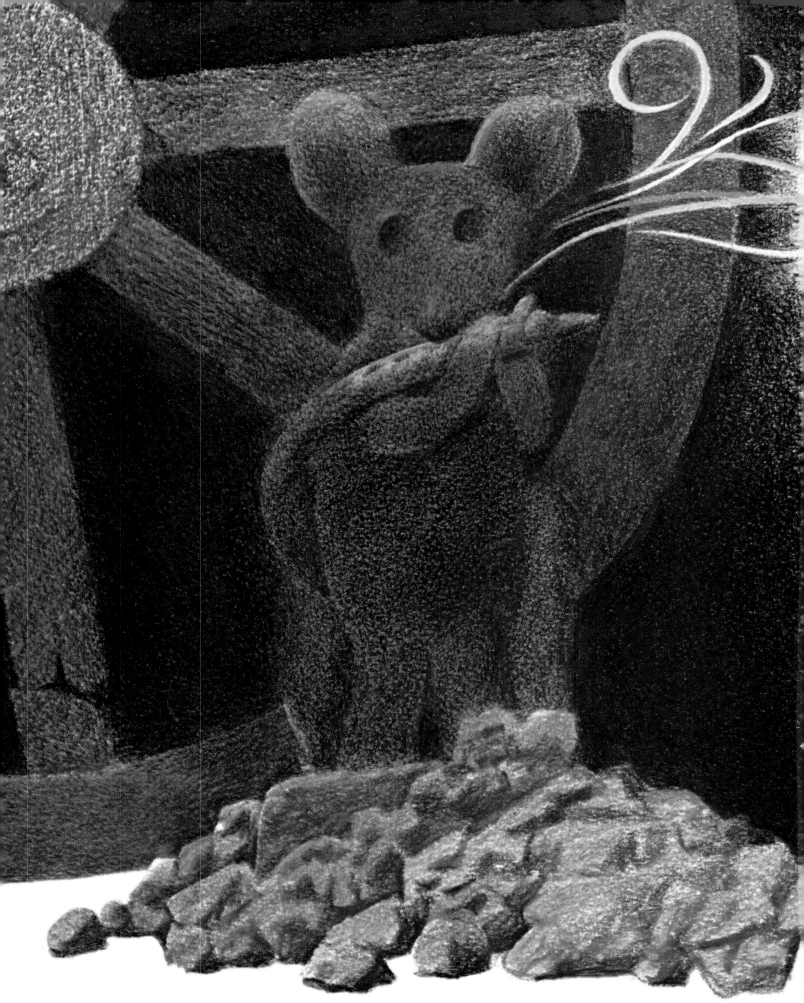

Then one day she met her friends on the street. They were desperate.

"Geraldine!" they said. "We have no more food, and there is none to be found anywhere. You must share your cheese with us."

"But that is not possible!" Geraldine shouted.

"Why?" asked the others angrily.

"Because . . . because . . . because it is MUSIC!"

Her friends looked at Geraldine, surprised. "What is music?" they asked all together.

For a moment Geraldine stood deep
in thought. Then she took a step backward,
solemnly lifted the tip of her tail to her puckered lips,
took a deep breath, and blew. She blew hard. She
puffed, she peeped, she tweeted, she screeched.
Her friends laughed until their hungry little
tummies hurt.

Then a long, soft, beautiful whistle came from Geraldine's lips. One of the melodies of the cheese flute echoed in the air. The little mice held their breath in amazement. Other mice came to hear the miracle. When the tune came to an end, Gregory, the oldest of the group, whispered, "If this is music, Geraldine, you are right. We cannot eat that cheese."

"No," said Geraldine joyfully. "Now we CAN eat the cheese. Because . . . now the music is in me."

With that they all followed Geraldine to the barn. And while Geraldine whistled the gayest of tunes, they ate cheese to their tummies' content.

Tico
and the
Golden Wings

*Many years ago I knew a little bird whose name was Tico. He would
sit on my shoulder and tell me all about the flowers, the ferns, and
the tall trees. Once Tico told me this story about himself.*

I don't know how it happened, but when I was young I had no wings.
I sang like the other birds and I hopped like them, but I couldn't fly.

   Luckily my friends loved me. They flew from tree to tree, and in the
evening they brought me berries and tender fruits gathered from the
highest branches.

   Often I asked myself, "Why can't I fly like the other birds? Why
can't I, too, soar through the big blue sky over villages and treetops?"

   And I dreamed that I had golden wings, strong enough to carry me
over the snow-capped mountains far away.

One summer night I was awakened by a noise nearby. A strange bird, pale as a pearl, was standing behind me.

"I am the wishingbird," he said. "Make a wish and it will come true."

I remembered my dreams and with all my might I wished I had a pair of golden wings. Suddenly there was a flash of light and on my back there were wings, golden wings, shimmering in the moonlight. The wishingbird had vanished.

Cautiously I flapped my wings. And then I flew. I flew higher than the tallest tree. The flower patches below looked like stamps scattered over the countryside, and the river like a silver necklace lying in the meadows. I was happy and I flew well into the day.

But when my friends saw me swoop down from the sky, they frowned on me and said, "You think you are better than we are, don't you, with those golden wings. You wanted to be *different*." And off they flew without saying another word.

Why had they gone? Why were they angry? Was it *bad* to be different? I could fly as high as the eagle. Mine were the most beautiful wings in the world. But my friends had left me and I was very lonely.

One day I saw a man sitting in front of a hut. He was a basket maker and there were baskets all around him.

There were tears in his eyes. I flew onto a branch from where I could speak to him.

"Why are you sad?" I asked.

"Oh, little bird, my child is sick and I am poor. I cannot buy the medicines that would make him well."

"How can I help him?" I thought. And suddenly I knew. "I will give him one of my feathers."

"How can I thank you!" said the poor man happily. "You have saved my child. But look! Your wing!"

Where the golden feather had been, there was a real black feather, as soft as silk.

From that day, little by little, I gave my golden feathers away and black feathers appeared in their place.

I bought many presents: three new puppets for a poor puppeteer, a spinning wheel to spin the yarn for an old woman's shawl, a compass for a fisherman who got lost at sea . . .

And when I had given my last golden feathers to a beautiful bride, my wings were as black as India ink.

I flew to the big tree where my friends gathered for the night. Would they welcome me?

They chirped with joy. "Now you are just like us," they said.

We all huddled close together. But I was so happy and excited, I couldn't sleep. I remembered the basket maker's son, the old woman, the puppeteer, and all the others I had helped with my feathers.

"Now my wings are black," I thought, "and yet I am not like my friends. We are *all* different. Each for his own memories, and his own invisible golden dreams."

Cornelius

When the eggs hatched, the little crocodiles crawled out onto the riverbeach. But Cornelius walked out *upright*.

As he grew taller and stronger he rarely came down on all fours. He saw things no other crocodile had ever seen before. "I can see far beyond the bushes!" he said.

But the others said, "What's so good about that?"

"I can see the fish from above!" Cornelius said.

"So what?" said the others, annoyed.

And so one day Cornelius angrily decided to walk away.

It was not long before he met a monkey. "I can walk upright!" Cornelius said proudly. "And I can see things far away!"

"I can stand on my head," said the monkey. "And hang from my tail."

Cornelius was amazed. "Could I learn to do that?" he asked.

"Of course," replied the monkey. "All you need is a lot of hard work and a little help."

Cornelius worked hard at learning the monkey's tricks, and the monkey seemed happy to help him. When he had finally learned to stand on his head and hang from his tail, Cornelius walked proudly back to the riverbeach.

"Look!" he said. "I can stand on my head."

"So what!" was all the others said.

"And I can hang from my tail!" said Cornelius.

But the others just frowned and repeated,

"So what!"

Disappointed and angry, Cornelius decided to go back to the monkey. But just as he had turned around, he looked back. And what did he see?

There the others were, falling all over themselves trying to stand on their heads and hang from their tails! Cornelius smiled. Life on the riverbeach would never be the same again.

Swimmy

A happy school of little fish lived in a corner of the sea somewhere.
They were all red. Only one of them was as black as a mussel shell.
He swam faster than his brothers and sisters.
His name was Swimmy.

One bad day a tuna fish, swift, fierce, and very hungry, came darting through the waves. In one gulp he swallowed all the little red fish.

Only Swimmy escaped. He swam away in the deep wet world. He was scared, lonely, and very sad.

But the sea was full of wonderful creatures, and as he swam from marvel to marvel Swimmy was happy again.

He saw a medusa made of rainbow jelly; a lobster, who walked about like a water-moving machine; strange fish, pulled by an invisible thread;

a forest of seaweeds growing from sugar-candy rocks; an eel whose tail was almost too far away to remember; and sea anemones, who looked like pink palm trees swaying in the wind.

Then, hidden in the dark shade of rocks and weeds, he saw a school of little fish, just like his own.

"Let's go and swim and play and SEE things!" he said happily.

"We can't," said the little red fish. "The big fish will eat us all."

"But you can't just lie there," said Swimmy. "We must THINK of something."

Swimmy thought and thought and thought. Then suddenly he said, "I have it! We are going to swim all together like the biggest fish in the sea!"

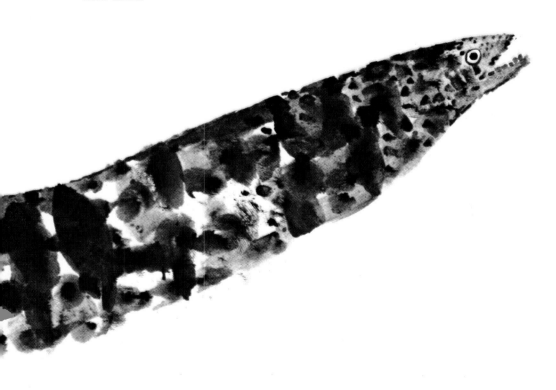

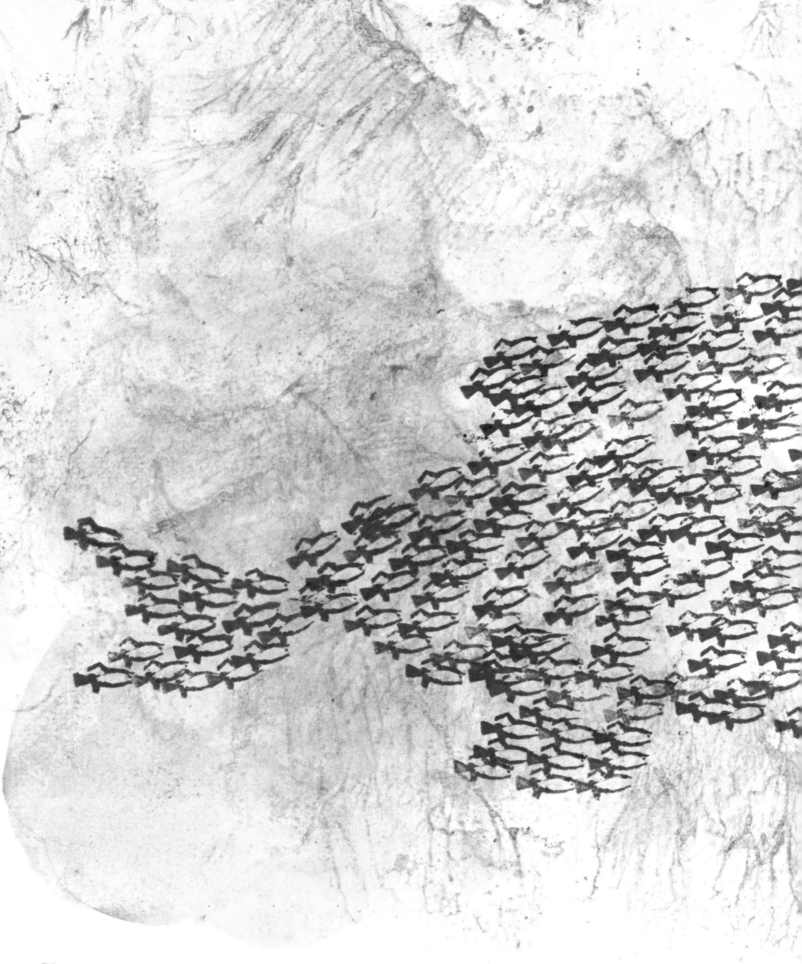

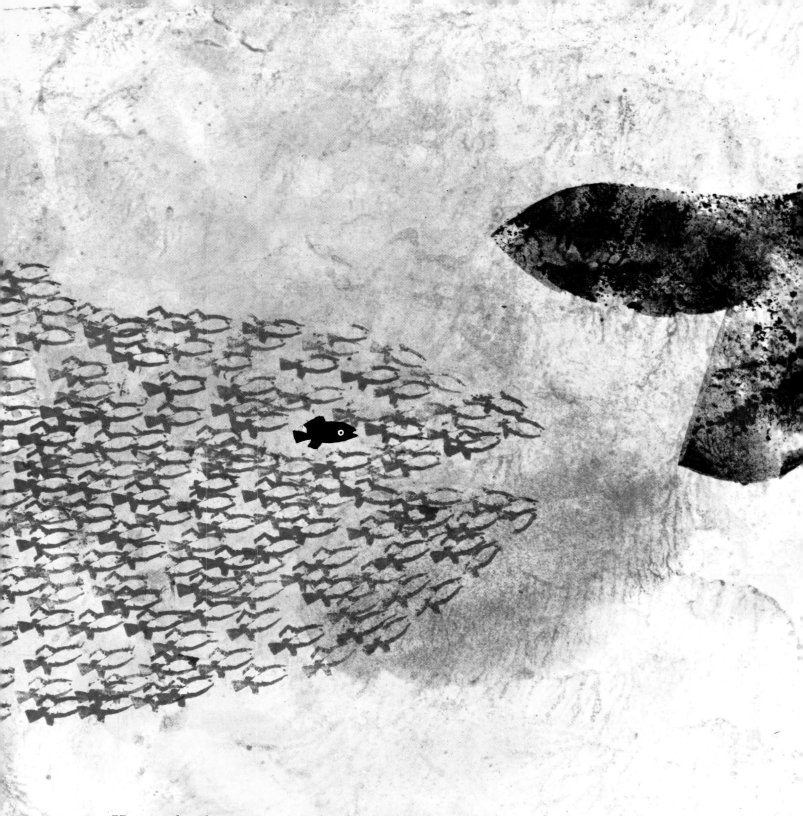

He taught them to swim close together, each in his own place,
and when they had learned to swim like one giant fish, he said,
"I'll be the eye."

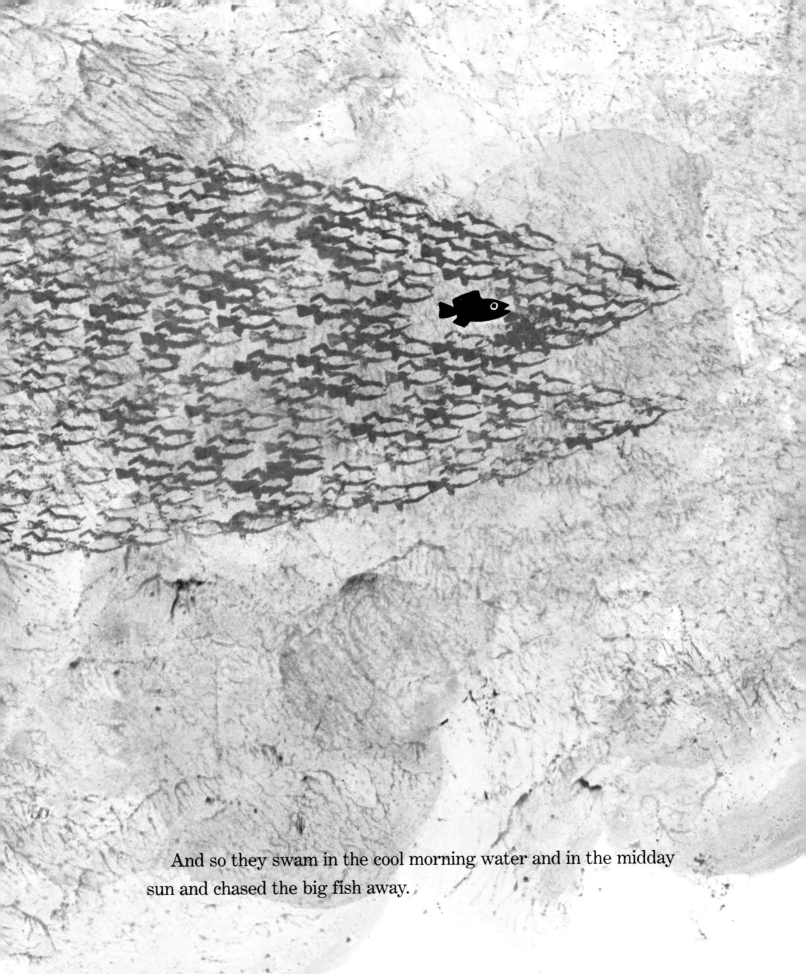

And so they swam in the cool morning water and in the midday
sun and chased the big fish away.

In the Rabbitgarden

The rabbitgarden was surely the most beautiful garden, and the two little rabbits the happiest bunnies, in the world.

One day the old rabbit called them. "I am going away for a while," he said in a raucous voice. "Behave well, and remember—eat all the carrots you want, but don't touch the apples or the fox will get you."

The two little rabbits ran back to play, and when they were hungry they dug up a carrot or two. The next day they dug here and they dug there, but they couldn't find a single carrot. "What will we do now?" they said, and tears came to their eyes.

Suddenly they saw a beautiful big carrot, half hidden by the trunk of an apple tree. They grabbed it eagerly, but—*whoops!*—it disappeared.

And there in front of them was an enormous serpent.

"Were you going to eat the tip of my tail?" he said. "Do little rabbits eat serpents nowadays?" And he laughed, "Ha! Ha! Ha!"

"Sorry," mumbled the bunnies, confused and a little scared. "We thought the tip of your tail was a carrot. We are hungry and there isn't a carrot to be found anywhere."

"Carrots, carrots," laughed the serpent. "With all the beautiful apples that hang in the apple tree!"

"We can't reach them," said the bunnies. "And besides—"

But before they could say "the old rabbit" the serpent presented them with the reddest, most fragrant apple they had ever seen or smelled. And was it good! When they had eaten their fill, the serpent said, "And now let's play!"

In the days that followed, the three became the best of friends. The serpent invented tricks and games. They rolled down slopes together, and he bounced them up into the air. And when they were hungry he picked them the ripest apples.

One morning the two little rabbits awoke with a jolt. There, peering out at them, half hidden in the weeds, was a big red fox. For a moment they felt as if they were frozen to the ground. Then they leaped for their lives. The fox followed close on their heels and was just about to catch them when . . .

there was the serpent waiting for them, his mouth wide open. The little rabbits understood at once. With a thump they plunged right into the serpent.

The fox had never seen such a fearful animal. "A dragon!" he cried. He turned around and ran right back where he had come from.

Then one fine day the old rabbit returned from his trip. He couldn't believe his eyes. Two happy little bunnies who ate apples! A smiling serpent! He was so surprised that he forgot to be angry.

The bunnies told him all about the serpent and how he had scared away the fox.

"Hmmm . . ." said the old rabbit, thinking about what he had heard.

Then the serpent picked the juiciest apple he could find.

"Okay," said the old rabbit, smiling. "Maybe apples are just big, round, shiny carrots that hang from carrot trees," and in a jiffy he gobbled up the apple, skin and all.

Theodore
and the
Talking Mushroom

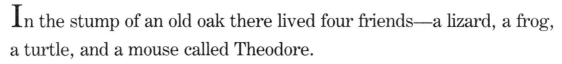

In the stump of an old oak there lived four friends—a lizard, a frog, a turtle, and a mouse called Theodore.

"Any time I lose my tail I can grow a new one," boasted the lizard.

"I can swim under water," said the frog.

"I can close like a box," said the turtle.

"And you?" they asked the mouse.

Theodore, who was always afraid, blushed. "I can run," he said.

The others laughed, "Ha! Ha! Ha!"

One day Theodore was frightened by a leaf that came fluttering down from a tree. "An owl!" he thought as he ran for cover.

Luckily he found a huge mushroom to hide under. He was too frightened to notice that it was as blue as an August sky. Theodore hid for a long time. He was tired. He had almost fallen asleep, when suddenly he was startled by a strange noise. "Quirp!"

Theodore looked around, his little heart beating wildly. But all was quiet. "I must have dreamed it," he thought as he returned to the cool shade of the mushroom. He dozed off softly, when suddenly there was that noise again—"Quirp!"

It was the mushroom! Theodore was too excited to be frightened. "Can you talk?" he gasped. The mushroom did not answer, but after a little while it made the noise again. And again. Soon Theodore realized that the mushroom could not really speak. It could only say "Quirp."

Then he had an idea.

He went back to his friends. "I have something important to tell you," he said mysteriously. "Some time ago I discovered a talking mushroom. The only one in the whole world. It is the Mushroom of Truth and I have learned to understand its language."

He guided his friends toward the edge of the woods. There stood the blue mushroom.

"Mushroom, speak!" Theodore commanded.

"Quirp!" said the mushroom.

"What does it mean?" asked Theodore's friends, dumbfounded.

"It means," said Theodore, "that the mouse should be venerated above all other animals."

"Quirp!"

The news of Theodore's discovery spread quickly. His friends made him a crown. Animals came from far away with garlands of flowers.

Theodore was no longer afraid. He did not have to run—he did not even have to walk. Wherever he went he was carried on the turtle's back on a cushion of flowers. And wherever he went he was venerated above all other animals.

One day he and his three friends went on a trip. They went far beyond
the edge of the woods through the fields of heather. There lay the hills they had
never crossed. The frog jumped ahead. Suddenly, from the top of the hill,

he shouted,

"Look! Look!"

The valley below was filled with hundreds of blue mushrooms!
And a chorus of "Quirps" filled the air.

"Quirp!"

"Quirp!"

"Quirp!"

"Quirp!"

"Quirp!"

"Quirp!"

"Quirp!"

"Quir

"Quirp!"

Speechless and bewildered, they all gaped at the unexpected sight. Theodore knew he should say something, but the words failed him and he just stood there trembling and stammering. Then his friends exploded with anger.

"Liar!" "Faker!" "Fraud!" they shouted.

"Charlatan!" "Scoundrel!" "Imposter!"

Theodore ran as he had never run before. Through the woods, past the blue mushroom, past the old oak stump . . .

He ran and ran. And his friends never saw him again.

A Color of His Own

Elephants are gray.
Goldfish are red.
Parrots are green.
Pigs are pink.

All animals have a color of their own, except chameleons. They change color wherever they go.

On lemons they are yellow.
In the heather they are purple.
And on the tiger they are striped like tigers.

One day a chameleon who was sitting on a tiger's tail said to himself, "If I remain on a leaf I shall be green forever, and so I too, will have a color of my own." With this thought he cheerfully climbed onto the greenest leaf.

But in autumn the leaf turned yellow—and so did the chameleon. Later the leaf turned red, and the chameleon, too, turned red. And then the winter winds blew the leaf from the branch and with it the chameleon.

The chameleon was black in the long winter night. But when spring came, he walked out into the green grass. And there he met another chameleon.

He told his sad story. "Won't we ever have a color of our own?" he asked.

"I'm afraid not," said the other chameleon, who was older and wiser. "But," he added, "why don't we stay together? We will still change color wherever we go, but you and I will always be alike."

And so they remained side by side.

They were green together,
and purple,
and yellow,

and red with white polka dots.

And they lived happily ever after.

The Greentail Mouse

In the quietest corner of the Willshire woods a community of field mice lived a peaceful life. There were sweet berries, juicy roots, and tender shoots to eat. The winter days were mild, and during the long summer a cool breeze played softly in the grass. No fox or snake ever discovered the hideout where the little friends had a fine time, day after day.

One spring morning a city mouse came passing through.

"Tell us all about the city," the field mice asked him.

"Most of the time it's sad and dangerous," he answered. "But there is one wonderful day."

"When?" asked the mice.

"Mardi Gras," said the city mouse with an air of mystery and importance. "That's French for Fat Tuesday. On Mardi Gras there is lots of music, and people dance in the streets." And he told them about parades, confetti, streamers, horns that make funny noises—and masks!

"Let's have a Fat Tuesday too!" exclaimed the mice excitedly.

That very afternoon they met at the big pebble. They all agreed that it would be nice to have a Mardi Gras. "We'll decorate the bushes, we'll have a parade and a ball, and at midnight we'll put on masks."

They worked and worked. They cut leaves into ribbons, which they hung from the low branches of trees and bushes. They gathered straw and lichens and petals and made masks of ferocious animals with glittering teeth and fierce eyes.

In the early evening they went to the place they had chosen for the big event. Most of them wore a wig or a hat, and one mouse had even painted her tail green.

"I am the Greentail Mouse," she said with a squeaky voice.

They danced and sang and had a wonderful time until the moon was at its highest point in the sky.

Then they disappeared into the dark bushes and put on their masks. From behind tree trunks and stones they scared each other with ferocious grunts and shouts and shrieks, and threatened each other with sharp teeth and tusks.

Little by little they forgot that they were sweet, harmless mice. They forgot about Mardi Gras and singing and dancing and being joyful. They *really* believed that they were ferocious animals.

"Waoo! Waoo!" yelled the Greentail Mouse from the branch onto which she had climbed.

Everyone was afraid of everyone else, and as the days went by, the once peaceful community became a place full of hate and suspicion.

One morning they saw a strange and frightening sight—*a mouse as tall as the elephant.* A giant mouse! At first they thought that it was a mouse masked as a mouse, but when they realized that it wore no mask at all, they were very frightened and ran as fast as they could. The mouse ran after them, and since he did not have the weight of a mask to carry, he easily overtook them.

"What are you afraid of?" he said. "Have you forgotten what a real mouse is like?"

"But you are the tallest mouse in the world! A giant mouse," the others said, still out of breath.

The mouse laughed. "Nonsense," he said. "If you take off those silly masks you will all be giant mice."

Timidly they removed their masks, one by one, and they realized that the mouse had been right. It was good to be themselves again—real mice, not afraid of one another and eager to have a happy time.

That night they decided to build a big fire and burn all the masks.

"This is better than Fat Tuesday," they said as the masks turned into ashes, and sparks of many colors rose into the sky.

By the time the fire had died out, no one would ever have suspected what had happened, for everything was the way it had been before.

Except for the Greentail Mouse. She just couldn't get her tail clean. She tried the rain and the water in the stream. She scratched and nibbled. She finally gave up. And when someone asked her why she had a green tail, she would shrug her shoulders and simply say, "I was the Greentail Mouse at Mardi Gras."

"What is Mardi Gras?" the other would ask.

"That's French for Fat Tuesday." And she would tell about parades, streamers, and horns that make funny noises. But she never said a word about the ferocious masks. They were tucked far away in her memory, almost forgotten, like a bad dream.

The Alphabet Tree

"This is the Alphabet Tree," said the ant.

"Why is it called the Alphabet Tree?" asked his friend.

"Because not so long ago this tree was full of letters. They lived a happy life, hopping from leaf to leaf on the highest twigs. Each letter had its favorite leaf, where it would sit in the sun and rock in the gentle breeze of spring.

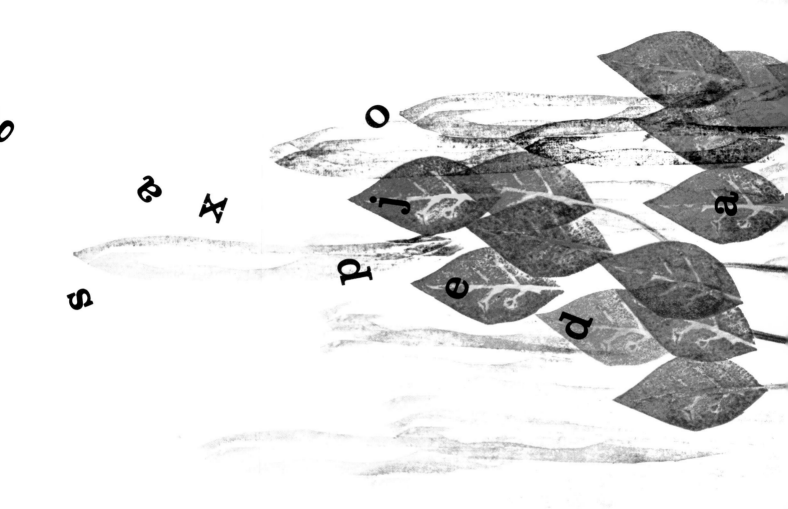

"One day the breeze became a strong gust and the gust became a gale. The letters clung to the leaves with all their might—but some were blown away, and the others were very frightened.

"When the storm had passed, they huddled together in fear, deep in the foliage of the lower branches.

"A funny bug, red and black with bright yellow wings, saw them there, hiding in the shade.

" 'We are hiding from the wind,' the letters explained. 'But who are you?'

" 'I am the word-bug,' the bug answered. 'I can teach you to make words. If you get together in threes and fours, and even more, no wind will be strong enough to blow you away.'

"Patiently he taught the letters to join together and make words. Some made short and easy words like *dog* and *cat*; others learned to make more difficult ones: *twig*, *leaf*, and even *earth*.

"Happily they climbed back onto the highest leaves, and when the wind came they held on without fear. The word-bug had been right.

"Then, one summer morning, a strange caterpillar appeared amid the foliage. He was purple, woolly, and very large. 'Such confusion!' said the caterpillar when he saw the words scattered around the leaves. 'Why don't you get together and make sentences—and *mean* something?'

"The letters had never thought of this. Now they could really write— *say* things. They said things about the wind, the leaves, the bug.

the wind is bad

leaves are green

the bug is small

" 'Good!' said the caterpillar approvingly.
'But not good enough.'

" 'Why?' asked the letters, surprised.

" 'Because you must say something *important*,'
said the caterpillar.

"The letters tried to think of something important, *really* important.
Finally they knew what to say. What could be more important than
peace? PEACE ON EARTH AND GOODWILL TOWARD ALL
MEN, they spelled excitedly.

" 'Great!' said the caterpillar. 'Now climb onto my back.'

will toward all men

"One by one the letters climbed onto the woolly back. 'But where are you taking us?' they asked anxiously as the caterpillar began climbing down the tree.

" 'To the President,' said the caterpillar."

132

Matthew's
Dream

A couple of mice lived in a dusty attic with their only child. His name was Matthew. In one corner of the attic, draped with cobwebs, were piles of newspapers, books, and magazines, an old broken lamp, and the sad remains of a doll. That was Matthew's corner.

The mice were very poor, but they had high hopes for Matthew. He would grow up to be a doctor, perhaps. Then they would have Parmesan cheese for breakfast, lunch, and dinner. But when they asked Matthew what he wanted to be, he said, "I don't know. . . . I want to see the world."

One day Matthew and his classmates were taken to the museum. It was the first time. They were amazed at what they saw. There was a huge portrait of King Mouse the Fourth, dressed like a general. And next to it was a picture of cheese that made Matthew drool. There were winged mice that floated through the air and mice with horns and bushy tails. And mountains and rushing streams, and branches bowing in the wind. The world is all here, thought Matthew.

Entranced, Matthew wandered from room to room gazing at the paintings. There were some that he didn't understand at first. One looked like crusts of pastry, but when he looked more carefully, a mouse emerged.

Then, turning a corner, Matthew found himself face to face with another little mouse. She smiled at him. "I am Nicoletta," she said. "Aren't these paintings wonderful?"

That night Matthew had a strange dream. He dreamed that he and Nicoletta were walking, hand in hand, in an immense, fantastic painting. As they walked, playful patches of color shifted under their feet, and all around them suns and moons moved gently to the sound of distant music. Matthew had never been so happy. He embraced Nicoletta. "Let's stay here forever," he whispered.

Matthew woke with a start. He was alone. Nicoletta had faded with his dream. The gray dreariness of his attic corner appeared to him in all its bleak misery. Tears came to his eyes.

But then, as if by magic, what Matthew saw began to change. The shapes hugged each other and the pale colors of the messy junk heap brightened. Even the crumpled newspapers now looked soft and smooth. And from afar Matthew thought he heard the notes of a familiar music.

He ran to his parents' corner. "I know!" he said. "Now I know! I want to be a painter!"

Matthew became a painter. He worked hard and painted large canvases filled with the shapes and colors of joy.

Then he married Nicoletta. In time he became famous, and mice from all over the world came to see and buy his paintings.

His largest painting now hangs in the museum. When asked about the title, Matthew smiles. "The title?" he says as if he had never thought about it before.

"My dream."

Six Crows

In a peaceful valley at the foot of the Balabadur Hills a farmer cultivated a field of wheat. The soil was fertile and the spring rains had been gentle.

Life would have been good and happy were it not for six noisy crows who nested in a tree nearby.

Just when the wheat was about to ripen, the crows descended upon the field and pecked away at the tender grains.

The farmer tried to chase the crows from the field. But no sooner had he returned to his hut than they were back. In desperation he built a scarecrow.

146

When the crows saw it standing in the wheat, waving a big stick, they were frightened. They huddled in their tree and wondered what to do. "We must scare that thing away!" they said. "But how?"

"Let's set the field on fire!" shouted a crow.

"But that would be the end of our wheat!" the others said.

There were many proposals. At last they agreed to make a ferocious kite. They gathered bark and dry leaves and made a fierce and very ugly bird.

The next morning they flew the kite over the field. The scarecrow didn't budge, but the farmer was very frightened. He ran into his hut and bolted the door tight. "I must build a scarier scarecrow," he said.

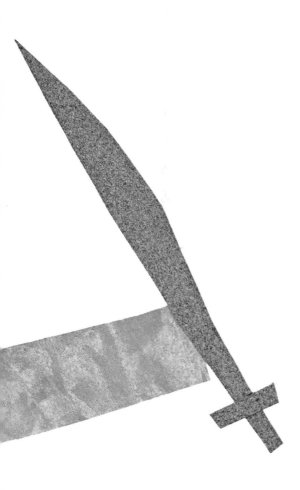

Soon a giant figure brandishing two swords stood in the wheat field. Its angry mouth seemed to grunt. "That should do it," said the farmer.

But when the crows saw the new menace, they gathered more bark and more leaves and built an even larger and more ferocious kite. They flew it over the field. Back and forth. The farmer was so scared that he didn't dare leave his hut.

From her nest in an old tree trunk an owl had been watching the goings-on. She shook her head. "I don't know who is sillier, the farmer or the crows," she thought.

When she noticed that the wheat was wilting from neglect, she decided to talk to the farmer. "Why don't you make peace, you and the crows?" she said.

"It's too late now," said the farmer angrily.

"It's never too late to talk things over," said the owl.

Then she went to see the crows.

"What can we do now?" asked the crows, dismayed when they heard that the wheat crop was in danger.

"Go and talk things over," said the owl. "Words can do magic."

The crows and the farmer agreed to meet near the owl's nest. While the owl looked on they talked and talked. First in anger, then more reasonably, finally like old friends.

"I must confess that I missed your happy cackling," said the farmer.

"And we missed your wheat!" said the crows. Soon they were laughing together.

"We must thank the owl," said the farmer. "But where is she?"

Her nest was empty. They looked all over.

They went to the field. There stood the giant scarecrow, but
something was different. The nasty grin had turned into a happy smile.
The owl was perched on the giant's arm. "What happened?" they asked.
"Magic," she said.

An
Extraordinary
Egg

On Pebble Island, there lived three frogs: Marilyn, August, and one who was always somewhere else.

That one's name was Jessica.

Jessica was full of wonder. She would go on long walks, way to the other side of Pebble Island, and return at the end of the day, shouting, "Look what I found!" And even if it was nothing but an ordinary little pebble, she would say, "Isn't it extraordinary?" But Marilyn and August were never impressed.

One day, in a mound of stones, she found one that stood out from all the others. It was perfect, white like the snow and round like the full moon on a midsummer night. Even though it was almost as big as she was, Jessica decided to bring it home.

"I wonder what Marilyn and August will say when they see this!" she thought as she rolled the beautiful stone to the small inlet where the three of them lived.

"Look what I found!" she shouted triumphantly. "A huge pebble!"

This time Marilyn and August were truly astonished. "That is not a pebble," said Marilyn, who knew everything about everything. "It's an egg. A chicken egg."

"A chicken egg? How do you know it's a chicken egg?" asked Jessica, who had never even heard of chickens.

Marilyn smiled. "There are some things you just know."

A few days later, the frogs heard a strange noise coming from the egg. They watched in amazement as the egg cracked and out crawled a long, scaly creature that walked on four legs.

"See!" exclaimed Marilyn. "I was right! It *is* a chicken!"

"A chicken!" they all shouted.

The chicken took a deep breath, grunted, gave each of the astonished frogs a look, and said in a small, raspy voice, "Where is the water?"

"Straight ahead!" the frogs cried out excitedly.

The chicken threw herself into the water, and the frogs dove in after her. To their surprise, the chicken was a good swimmer, and fast too, and she showed them new ways to float and paddle. They had a wonderful time together and played from sunup to sundown.

And so it went for many days.

Then, one day, when Jessica was somewhere else, August and Marilyn saw a commotion in the water below them. Someone was in trouble. Quickly, the chicken dove into the dark pool. August and Marilyn were frightened.

After a few long moments, the chicken reappeared, carrying Jessica. "I'm all right," she called. "I got tangled in the weeds, but the chicken saved me."

From that day on, Jessica and her rescuer were inseparable friends. Wherever Jessica went, the chicken went too. They traveled all over the island. They went to Jessica's secret thinking place and to the great pebble monument.

One day they went to a place where Jessica had never been before. A red and blue bird flew down from a tree.

"Oh, there you are!" it exclaimed when it saw the chicken. "Your mother has been looking all over for you! Come! I'll take you to her."

They followed the bird for a very long time. They walked and they walked. They walked under the warm sun and the cool moon, and then they came upon the most extraordinary creature they had ever seen.

It was asleep. But when it heard the little chicken shout "Mother!" it slowly opened one eye, smiled an enormous smile, and, in a voice as gentle as the whispering grass, said, "Come here, my sweet little alligator." And the little chicken climbed happily onto her mother's nose.

"Now it's time for me to go," said Jessica. "I'll miss you very much, little chicken. Come visit us soon— and bring your mother too."

Jessica couldn't wait to tell Marilyn and August what had happened. As she neared the inlet, she shouted, "Guess what I found!" And she told them all about it. "And do you know what the mother chicken said to her baby?" Jessica asked. "She called her 'my sweet little alligator'!"

"Alligator!" said Marilyn. "What a silly thing to say!"

And the three frogs couldn't stop laughing.